Hidden Secrets

By
Jasmine Barton-Moore

An Imprint of Jasmine Barton-Moore Publishing House
Copyright © 2017 Jasmine Barton-Moore
All rights reserved.

ISBN number 978-0-9991789-3-5 Paperback
ISBN number 978-0-9991789-2-8 ebook
www.jasminebartonmoorepublishinghouse.com

Hidden Secrets

He moved down to her hidden treasure and placed his mouth there. He licked over her clit and put his tongue inside of her. He began speeding up. He could feel her on the verge of climaxing. That's when he removed his mouth, climbed on top of her, removed the wrapper from the condom and covered his shaft. He kissed her on the lips and entered inside of her. Malachi froze, it couldn't be possible. He looked down at Kim. Her face showed no expression. "Kim, are you a virgin?"

Jasmine Barton-Moore

Contents

Jasmine Barton-Moore

Dear reader,

Thank you to all my readers. When you think you can't do it, remember you can.

-I am strong when I am weak!
Tasha Cobbs

Jasmine Barton-Moore

Acknowledgments

I want to start off by acknowledging the self-publishing community. The time and effort put into writing a book is a lot of work. I would like to thank the people who have helped me design the cover, edit, and format. All my readers, family, and friends who continue to support me.

Jasmine Barton-Moore

Preface

She had to move. They were catching up to her once again. As she quickly packed her bags with all of her belongings, she was thinking of a new place to move to. She checked her duffle bag making sure she had her most value possessions. Her little black book was her key to freedom, just in due time. As she rushed out of the motel, she could hear voices near the elevator, so she ran in the opposite direction toward the staircase. She kept looking over her shoulder as she hurried inside the taxi that would bring her straight to the Greyhound. It would be less difficult for her to be tracked. There was no time for her to waste. As she arrived at the Greyhound station, she purchased a ticket for the next bus that would be leaving in ten minutes. Her next destination would be Atlanta, Georgia.

* * *

"Boss we lost her again, she is not in the motel room anymore. It looks like she just gotten, out of the shower, and the coffee pot is still on."

"Well, you find her. And do it quickly."

"Yes sir, I'm top of it." He ended the phone call.

Kim was finally on the bus. She was exhausted, most of the time she hardly ever slept. She was departing from Los Angeles, so she would be on the Greyhound for the next three days. At her next stop, she was planning on changing her appearance. At the moment she was covered in black from head to toe. She was also wearing a long black wig. One of her favorite wigs from her collection. She couldn't recall the last time her natural hair was out and free. Often times she felt that her life SUCKED. Fortunately, she knew that if she ever wanted to live in a world where she could live freely, then she would first have to get justice.

She leaned back in her chair, trying to relax a little bit. Kim thought back to the time where she was just nineteen and she found out that her mother had lied about not knowing her biological father. So, Kim went looking for him. After her long journey to finding him, she was shocked found that he was not very pleased to see her. Her biological father told her mother to get an abortion, but she refused. Kim was absolutely heartbroken as she heard those words. How could a man not want their own flesh and blood? She drove home crying; she didn't want to upset her mom, so she never told her what had happened that day. As she looked back on her life, she often wondered what her mother's reactions and feelings would have been if she had told her the truth. Would she be alive today?

It was the middle of the night when her mom had come to her and put her hands over Kim's mouth. "Kim don't make any noises, just listen. I need you to take your sister and leave right now. No matter what happens, do not turn back. Don't come back for me."

"Mom what is going on?"

"Kim, I don't have time to explain any of this right now. In this envelope you will find a letter explaining everything. There are also passports, new identities, and money. I just need you to promise me that you won't come back. Now go and grab your sister. Remember that closet that I always tell you not to go into? Well, tonight is the night you can finally go inside. It will lead you out of the house and onto the main road. There, you will find a car. It has a full tank of gas, blankets and a cell phone. There is only one number on that phone. And it's the only one you need to call. So, call the number and then listen carefully to their instructions. Kim, I'm sorry. Please don't forget, I love you."

Kim looked into her mom's frightened eyes as her mom leaned in to give her a kiss on the forehead before she left the room. Kim took the envelope and threw on some sweatpants and a sweatshirt. She rushed over to the end of the hall as she grabbed her sister. She then instructed her sister to toss on her own sweatpants and sweatshirt. They snuck out of the house through the secret passage that her mother had specifically installed.

Kim was scared as they made their way through the tunnel and into the car. Kim didn't even know about the tunnel or the car. Kim never understood, until now. Kim unlocked the car door and opened it for her sister. She then climbed in the front and put the key in the ignition and turned it. But Kim couldn't drive she needed to see what was happening. "I'll be right back," Kim said.

"Please Kim, don't leave me. It's dark out here."

"Give me five minutes," Kim handed her sister her watch. "When the clock strikes two o' clock, I will be back in the car with you."

Kim headed back toward the tunnel that led back into the house. Even though she was told never to come back, something just didn't feel right with her leaving her mother behind. Kim made it back to the house, but she made sure to be quiet. She could hear voices coming from the living room. As she peeked around the corner toward the living room, she was in shock as she saw her mom tied up to a chair. She recognized the man that was standing in front of her; it was her father. Plus it was two other men with him, but she had never seen them before. The same man that she went to see just a week prior.

"You know Ava, I asked you to get an abortion for a reason. That daughter of ours daughter came to pay me a little visit. From my understanding, a daughter that never was to exist.

Kim glanced over at her mother again. There was no sign of fear on her face or body language. She simply just said, "You don't get to decide what I do with my body." At that moment Kim's mom made eye contact with her. As she motioned her to leave, with her eyes moving from Kim back to the tunnel. Kim stayed glued to the floor.

"Once I find that daughter of ours, I am going to kill her just like how I am about to kill you." And just like that, he pointed the gun at Ava's temple and pulled the trigger. Kim still could not budge. All she could do was cover her mouth to muffle the scream that escaped from her throat.

"Search the whole house until you find her, and when you do, kill her!"

"Yes boss."

That was Kim's cue to get the hell out of there. As Kim made her way back into the car, she couldn't help but just stare blankly into her sister's eyes. Kim held back her tears as she started the engine. She felt a strong emotion of guilt as she drove away. "Kim is everything alright? Where's mommy?" Ava asked.

Kim looked at Ava through the mirror and immediately looked away. What she couldn't understand was why her father went through such great lengths of tracking them down, just to kill her mother.

Jasmine Barton-Moore

Chapter 1

KIM WOKE UP, STARTLED, AS THE BUS came to a stop. They were parked on the side of the road. She heard the bus driver speaking. "Sorry folks, it looks like we have a flat tire, but we should be up and running within the hour." Kim started to panic a little, thinking that the tire was deliberately sabotaged, but she knew that it wasn't possible. Kim turned to face the gentleman sitting next to her. "Excuse me, sir, do you know where we are?" He told her that they were in Phoenix, Arizona. That instantly put Kim at ease. Just like the bus driver had promised, they were back on the road again within the hour. And their next stop would be New Mexico where she could finally eat -- she had slept through the first stop.

It was early Friday morning when they finally arrived in New Mexico. Kim noticed a Denny's inside the bus station, but just to be safe she had to make sure to change her appearance before she ordered food. As she walked into the bathroom, she noticed a mother and daughter bonding. It made her think of her mother and how she missed her family so badly. She remembered that no matter how old she was her mom always insisted on going in the bathroom with her. But now was not the time or place because it would just place them in harm's way. Not until after she put her father behind bars for what he did. She entered the stalls and removed each article of clothing. She then slipped into an all black outfit. She also changed out of her long wig for a short brown bob wig with a part down the middle. She also added a pair of glasses to complete the look. When she was all done, she walked over to the sink to wash her hands. She looked at herself in the mirror and saw the reflection of this young twenty-four year old looking back at her, she was tired of running. She wished she could just find one detective that was willing to help her. Even though this trip was a last minute decision, she remembered overhearing that there were still decent cops on the force in the ATL. Everywhere she had gone her father had someone he could pay off. This was the closest they had ever gotten to capturing her. At her next stop she couldn't be as careless. Before this nightmare began, she attended one of the best schools in Beverly Hills. All she wanted to do was return to Rolling Hills College and finish her degree in engineering. Her brain was brilliant, all she needed was a computer and she could hack into anything because she was naturally great with numbers. That was one of the reasons she was on the run. She had done research on her father and found out what kind of business he owned. She knew with a brain like hers he would probably have her laundering money and hacking into police stations. Kim reached into her duffel bag to retrieve the letter her mother handed her before forcing her into the tunnel. She read:

Dear Kim,

As I write this I had hoped that it would never come to this. When I met your father, he wined and dined me like no man has ever done before. Then I had gotten pregnant with you and he wanted me to give you up, and I just couldn't bring myself to do that. I was willing to stay in the same state as him, but I witnessed him killing someone. So I brought you into this world as a secret. He was never supposed to know about you. I believe he wanted me to get an abortion at the time because he was a married man. I knew it was wrong, but I just wanted to be loved. When you reached the age of five, I knew that I had a gifted daughter because you were able to do things that no child in your class was capable of. To ensure your safety, I created a fake birth certificate, making you a whole year younger. You will not be safe until your twenty-fifth birthday. Lastly, your grandmother set up your trust fund. Meaning if your father was to attempt killing you or capturing you he will be the next of kin to get the money. My sweet angel, be safe and I love you.

Love, Mom

Kim would be twenty-five in a short span of six months. Even though it was almost her birthday, she just didn't feel a sense of joy. Kim wiped the tears from her eyes and walked out of the bathroom. She grabbed herself a bite to eat before getting back on the bus. As she was making her way onto the bus, she could feel the bus driver just staring at her. Kim had gotten use to this, especially with the different identities that she had to carry.

Kim sat back down in her seat and thought about her sister. She remembered placing her sister on a plane so that she could go live with her aunt in Paris. She told her sister that she would sometimes visit, but she hadn't seen her sister since the night she put her on the plane. She would sometimes call her, but that was all. She sent her sister a matching bracelet. That was about four years ago. Kim and her sister didn't have the same father; her stepfather passed away from lung cancer, but he was a great stepfather to her because he never treated her any differently. She stopped thinking about her family and looked toward the present. They would be in Atlanta by morning, so she decided to get some shut eye.

* * *

James couldn't believe Ava had his child. Then to find out she was brilliant smart. He had her school records in front of him; at the age of nineteen, she was already working on her PhD in engineering. He has no intentions of harming her. He just wanted to make sure her mom said nothing about that night. But she was making it difficult for him to keep her out of harm's way. She kept trying to get any police department on her side for her mother's death. He wanted her to work for him. In his line of work, he could use a person like her on his staff; she was a walking computer. He knew he was being selfish, but that was part of his job. Taking what he wanted when he wanted to. He knew that she was trying to get him charged for her mother's death, but he could pretty much go anywhere and get any cop on his payroll. All he had to do was offer the right amount money, and if that didn't work, he would threaten them and their families. There was a knock on the door.

"Come in."

"We couldn't find her sir. She has outsmarted us once again," said his employee. As he said that he rocked back and forth from one foot to the other. And looked at his partner next to him. He was nervous as to what was coming next.

He stood up from his chair and pointed his gun at the men who worked for him. He pulled the trigger and shot the guy right in the arm. "You think I don't know that, you idiot?" The man let out a scream.

"Now go get yourself cleaned up, you're bleeding all over my floor. And when you're done, come back so we can think of a strategy to capture Kimberly Ann." The men left the room and James went back to plotting. He couldn't figure out just how she knew that he had murdered her mother. His men had searched the house and they came up with nothing. He couldn't help but think that once he had Kim he would be even more rich and powerful. With her skills and his connections. He remembered when he met Ava. She was working in the hospital as a front desk clerk. He just couldn't keep his eyes off of her. She was drop dead gorgeous. He asked her out that same day. At first she was hesitant but then she said yes. After that first night he knew he was addicted to her, but at the time he was married. He didn't believe in getting a divorce. His wife was ill, so he constantly took care of her medical bills. They never had kids themselves, so it came as a shock when he found out about Kim. His affair with Ava went on for about two years before she got pregnant and disappeared, after he had asked her to get an abortion. He never wanted children but come to find out she never got the abortion. He rubbed his hand down his face in frustration. "My men will catch her." He said out loud.

Chapter 2

KIM HEARD THE BUS DRIVER ANNOUNCE that they finally arrived in Atlanta, Georgia. She was grateful and relieved because being on a Greyhound bus for three days was just crazy. Kim grabbed her bags as she proceeded to call for a taxi.

Kim decided this time she wanted to stay at a mom and pop hotel, just because it would be a little harder to find her. She pulled up to a hotel that read Joan's Bed & Breakfast. As Kim stepped out of the taxi, she felt the urge to change her attire. It was the middle of June and it was one hundred and five degrees, and her all black just wouldn't cut it. She knew Atlanta would be hot, but she didn't expect it to be this hot. She paid the cab driver and went inside to check in.

When she entered, she was welcomed by an older lady across the counter. It was warm and cozy, and it smelled of fresh brewed coffee. There were beige couches with red pillows. The walls were painted a nice shade of tan. Everything about the place said, "Welcome home," and she instantly fell in love with it.

"Hello dear, are you checking in?"

"Yes ma'am, my name is Kimberly Parker." Parker wasn't her real last name. She tried to stick to the truth as much as possible. Kim handed over her identification card as she paid for the room in cash. Like always.

"Thank you Kimberly, here is your room key. You will be on the second floor. Complimentary breakfast is from six am to ten thirty am. There is a laundry facility on the first floor, it is twenty-four hours access and you can purchase your detergent across the street at the mini mart. And here is a list of places to eat at and tourist spots. How long will you be staying with us?"

Kim didn't like her full name. "You can call me Kim, and thank you for all of this. That gives me enough time to change and come back down and enjoy breakfast. Also, I am not too sure yet ma'am."

Mrs. Joan smiled. "Oh dear, if I get to call you Kim then you can call me Joan. Enjoy your stay, Kim."

Kim entered into her room. There was a queen size bed with a balcony view overlooking the parking lot area so she could see who was coming and who was leaving. Everywhere she stayed she had to make sure she had an escape plan. The bathroom was spacious, too. After she set up her own security systems and tapped into the hotel's, she called Tommy Brown.

She and Tommy went all the way back to when

they were five years old. She remembered begging her mom to go to a neighborhood school and not some prep school. That's when she met Tommy. She was sitting down at the lunch tables when a bunch of kids were standing around him and teasing him about having different colored socks along with his dirty shoes. Kim approached those kids and stood up for Tommy. He told her that she didn't have to do that as he walked away. She thought she had done him a favor. The very next day, he decided to sit next to her during lunch. They went through school being each other's best friend, even though she finished school early. He was like the brother she never had. He always had her back no matter what. They kept in touch, but not like before because she didn't want anything to happen to him. She would call him occasionally just letting him know she was still alive. He wanted to do so much more, to help her out but she couldn't afford to lose him too. The phone rang again before he picked up.

"Hello Tommy." Tommy had this deep voice. He was a tall, muscular white guy on the outside, but on the inside he was one of the brothers.

"Kim, where are you now? I tried calling your room in Los Angeles, but there was no answer."

"Yes Tommy, somehow they found me again."

Tommy heard Kim sigh, then asked "Well, where are you?"

"I plan to keep that bit of information to myself

just in case something happens." It wasn't that Kim didn't trust Tommy; she just didn't want him and his family in danger. She did a little research about a cop family here. It wasn't by coincidence that she was in Atlanta. Even though she picked the fastest bus out of LA, she had already began researching Atlanta prior to arriving.

"Okay Kim, be safe and make sure you calling to check in."

"I will Tommy."

Kim got off the phone with Tommy and hopped in the shower.

Chapter 3

KIM WALKED OUT HER DOOR AND DOWN the stairs to the breakfast area. She entered and it appeared as though no one was there. She was a little bit happy about that just because she didn't feel like having conversation at the moment. She scanned over the breakfast buffet bar as she grabbed a plate and filled it with smothered potatoes, pancakes, bacon, and eggs with cheese. She sat her food down on the table and went back for her syrup and coffee. She sat down in her seat and looked around. She really enjoyed this family owned business hotel. She sat at a huge round table that could fit probably thirty people. Kim said grace and bit into the potatoes. She hadn't had a home cooked meal in quite some time now. She heard a lot of commotion in the hallway and immediately walked in eight people. They all had similar features in their faces that stood out. There eyes were all the same. She could tell that they were related. They all grabbed plates and just started piling up their plates, not even noticing that she was there.

"Save some food for my guests now," she heard

Mrs. Joan say.

"Aunt Joan all your guests have eaten, it's almost clean up time." This came from an older gentleman as he chuckled.

"Well, there is a guest right there." Joan pointed at Kim.

Kim didn't know what to say. That was the thing about her, she liked things to be planned out. She hated being put on the spot. "Oh, that's fine Mrs. Joan. I can go up to my room and eat."

"That is nonsense Kim. This here is my family they like to stop by and take my free food on their way to work. This is my brother in law Malachi Hopkins Sr. This is my lovely sister-in-law Katherine Hopkins, and she comes by to help me run this place from time to time. And these are their four kids Malik, Malachi Jr, Terrell, and Nia."

"Nice to meet you all." The one they called Malachi just kept staring at her. There was something about him that drew her into his eyes. He had dark brown eyes, but before she could really study him, someone said something to her.

"What brings you to Atlanta, Kim?"

It was Nia who asked her the question. It looked as if they could be the same age. "I have never been to Atlanta, so I wanted to take the chance to explore it."

"That's awesome, maybe I can show you around and be your tour guide."

"Jeez Nia, can you say stalker much." This came from Terrell. Everyone busted out laughing.

"Shut up Terrell. Do you mind Kim? It's rare we get young people staying here."

Nia was an attractive woman. They were all attractive with their chocolate creamy skin. "No not at all, here is my number."

"Awesome, my dad is the chief of police. My two brothers Malik and Malachi are also on the force. Malik is the captain of his own precinct and Malachi is a detective at the same precinct. My younger brother here Terrell is a firefighter. He took a different route and I am fresh out of law school." They sat down at the table with her.

Kim choked a little bit, but not where it was noticeable. This was the family she had read about. Who knew she would be introduced to them so soon. This could be good and bad for her. She could finally get help on her mother's case, but she just lied to everyone in the room about who she really was. She planned to do some research on them later.

"What do you do for work Kim?"

Everyone just stared at Kim. She didn't know what to say. She just stared at them. Luckily, Mrs. Joan stepped in. "Stop harassing my guest and let her finish her breakfast in peace."

Several phones began to ring, and instantly the table started to clear. As everyone was leaving Malachi stole a last glance at her, then he finally turned around and left.

Kim couldn't put her finger on it, Malachi was an attractive man, but she couldn't really explain her feelings for him considering she had never been with a man before. She finished eating her food and headed back up to her room to take a nap. It had been a long three days.

Chapter 4

MALACHI SAT AT HIS DESK WORKING on paperwork as he waited for his partner to get in. He couldn't concentrate much. There was something about Kim that he just couldn't shake. He didn't know if it was because of the way she smiled at him. Malachi hadn't been attracted to a woman in a while. Yes, there had been certain women who have caught his eye, but nothing went beyond that. He was sitting at his computer in deep thought when his partner arrived.

"Hey partner, what you working on there?"

He and Willow had been partners for about three years now. "Working on paperwork for the case we closed two days ago. You know it was your turn to write it up."

"Ah come on Malachi, you know that I hate paperwork. I promise I owe you big time." As she sat down at her desk.

"That's what you said the last time, this time I am going to hold you to it." Malachi chuckled; he knew Willow hated doing paperwork, she described it as a waste of time. They caught the bad guy, so what was there to write. He had agreed with her up to a certain extent, but of course they needed it logged in as evidence just in case it went to trial. He looked at Willow. She was an attractive woman, but he was not attracted to her. Willow was a petite Native American woman. She always kept her hair in a low bun at the nape of her neck. She had a personality that drew everyone to her, but if you got on her bad side, that was a different story.

Willow sat at her desk and sipped her coffee. "Hey "Malachi, what is going on in the Captain's office?"

"You know Willow, just because my brother is captain of this precinct and my father is chief of police doesn't mean I know every detail on every case."

"Now that is a load of bull. Plus you know I like your brother, he is so damn fine."

Before Malachi could respond to Willow's comment, the Captain called them into his office. The Captain kept his office plain and simple. A few pictures of family here and there. When entering the room Malachi noticed the women standing there. She was wearing a matching pant suit. Her hair was loose around her face. Her eyes looked trouble but she forced a smile at them. She was an attractive Caucasian women, but not really his type of women. He was always observant.

"Detectives, you already know the chief. I would like to introduce you to agent Athena Burns, FBI. This is detective Malachi Hopkins and detective Willow Fox."

"FBI, wow. What are you guys doing all the way down here in Atlanta?"

"Willow," both Captain and Malachi said at the same time.

"What, everyone was thinking it. Nice to meet you Agent Burns, how can we help?"

"We believe that one of the major crime bosses from Los Angeles has some of his men on their way here. We don't know what he is looking for, but what we do know is that he is searching for someone. His name is James Cunningham. You may have heard of him before."

Everyone in the room looked at each other. They knew who she was talking about. "What makes you think he's here?" Willow asked.

Agent Burns pulled out a map. "We have been trying to catch James for three years now. He has committed several crimes up and down the state of California. Last year we began noticing him doing more business on the east coast. Every time we build a case on him, evidence magically gets lost and witnesses begin to disappear. My team has been tracking his every move, we even have someone on the inside. I don't know what brings him to Atlanta, but I know for a fact that he is looking for something or somebody. Back in LA we found some of his people poking around in a hotel room that was ram shacked, but by the time we arrived there was no one on site. The hotel manager was the one who notified the police. The only thing the hotel manager could tell us was there was a young woman staying there, but the manager had never seen her face before, so he couldn't give us a description."

"Were there no other employees? How did she pay?" Willow said, interrupting again.

"This hotel was set up in a way where you could rent and pay for your room online. We traced the woman's credit card, but it came back as a fake identity."

"So, why are you here?" Malachi asked.

"Detective Hopkins, we have reason to believe that the woman James is searching for is here. I say that because James has bought an airplane ticket to come out here in a few weeks. We monitor anytime he leaves the state or the country. Since this is your state, I wanted help from locals who know the area; a fresh pair of eyes on the case. Plus, you have done well in your career."

Malachi and Willow looked at each other. He knew what that look was. They got the vibe that agent Burns wasn't telling the whole story, and that made him want to be on the case that much more. Usually the FBI never used locals on cases. Especially a high case profile like this. "Okay we're in, show us everything you got."

Chapter 5

MALACHI HAD A LONG DAY AT THE OFFICE going over multiple files with Burns and Willow. It was insane how the same man could keep getting away with multiple crimes over and over again without ever getting caught. From murder, to tampering with evidence. Making witnesses disappear. Drugs. He had everything on his wrap sheet. He finally arrived home. Malachi walked over to the fridge and pulled out a beer. All he could think about was Kim. Her skin was a creamy mocha. Her olive shaped dark brown eyes. Her straight shoulder length hair that flowed freely. He could tell her hair was a wig, but she looked damn good in it. Not a lot of women could pull off that type of wig and make it look natural. He pictured her once again in her army green dress that hugged her curves. At least that's what he could tell by her sitting down. He couldn't really see what her body looked like considering that she was sitting down but he could see her full breast and that she wasn't wearing a bra. When it was time to head out, he had to take a moment to sit a bit longer, trying to control his other head. He needed a cold shower.

Just as he turned off the lights in the kitchen, his phone rang. He looked at the caller ID and saw that it was his aunt Joan calling. "Hello my beautiful aunt, how may I be of service to you tonight?" Malachi chuckled, he loved his aunt to death. He made sure to always be there for her, especially when her husband passed away last year.

"Oh Malachi stop it, you're such a sweet man. Why do you treat this old woman so well?"

"Because I have a great, beautiful aunt." Malachi could hear her chuckling.

"I know tomorrow is your day off, but I was wondering if you could stop by and help me fix some of the broken light bulbs in some of the rooms?"

Malachi wanted to say no so bad. He just wanted to relax, but he could never deny his aunt. Matter of fact he could deny none of the women in his family that's why they always called him first. "Of course I can help, what if I stop by around noon?"

"That sounds great Malachi, thank you."

* * *

Aunt Joan hung up the phone. She had seen the way Malachi looked at her guest Kim, so she was going to play a little matchmaking. She knew that after his messy divorce, he had never truly returned to his old self or dating. But she saw a spark in his eyes as he looked at Kim.

* * *

Kim woke up in her room a little startled. For a moment she had forgotten where she was. She stretched, got out of bed and went straight to her computer. Kim was good at what she did, all she needed was a computer and she could hack into anything. She wanted to check the premises and get into their computer system. After breakfast that day, she did some wandering around. She even put cameras outside her room, in the hallway, the stairways, in the lobby, and even the dining area, plus outside. She would extend the perimeter once it got dark. That's how she was able to stay one step ahead of her father. After she was done checking the cameras, she logged into her computer and searched for more information on the Hopkins. Everyone in their family was either a cop, firefighter, lawyer, or a retiree. Kim wanted to stay here just to see how the Hopkins' family operated. She knew that her father could buy off any cop if he wanted to, and she was running out of states and options. She decided to stay, but would just have to be more cautious.

She got off the computer and walked over to the window. It was evening time and it was starting to get dark. She needed it to be pitch-black so she could work out her exit strategies if it ever came down to that. Kim looked out the window some more as she wondered what her life would have been if things had turned out a bit differently.

* * *

It was finally pitch-black outside. Kim dressed in her all black from head to toe. She opened up her duffle bag and began to pull out small cameras. She purchased these special made cameras from a guy online. They were top of the line stuff; small like a button and they picked up audio and video very well. She made sure she had everything she needed before she left her room. After she was done expanding the perimeters, she went back to her room to shower and have a snack. Kim looked at the clock and it was almost one am. She thought about her sister and wondered how she was doing. It wasn't safe for them to be together right now, but she still managed to check in with her daily, now that she was a little bit older. Kim was exhausted, she was tired of running and not being able to live her life the way she wanted.

As she began to close her eyes, an image of Malachi popped in her mind. She could get use to looking at him. She had never dated before. She had kissed a boy once, but that was all. With her lifestyle it was hard to be romantic with someone, and guys in college were mad that she was smarter and wiser than them. Plus, at the time she wasn't of age anyway. Malachi was nicely built, he had broad shoulders, he was tall, had a square jaw line, lips that she wanted to get lost in. Kim started to feel a tingle down south. She opened her eyes so quick. Is this what it meant to be attracted to someone? Because she could get use to this. She closed her eyes again and started dreaming of Malachi.

Jasmine Barton-Moore

Chapter 6

WHEN KIM WOKE UP, IT WAS a Saturday morning and she had the urge to explore. But first, she needed breakfast. After breakfast yesterday she was excited to eat the food again. She hadn't had a home cook meal since her mom passed away. Kim dressed in her usual all black outfit, but this time a dress since it was hot outside. She had also decided to leave the wig off today and let her curls free. She went downstairs, and as soon as she walked in she saw Mrs. Joan and Malachi chatting away. He looked like he had just sat down because his plate looked like it hadn't been touched.

Ms. Joan smiled when she noticed Kim. "Good morning Kim, how did you sleep?"

Kim picked up a plate and began putting food on it while speaking to Joan at the same time. "Good morning Joan, and I slept well thanks for asking."

"Hey Kim, you remember my nephew Malachi?"

"Yes I remember him, good morning Malachi." "Good morning Kim."

"Do you have any plans for today?" Mrs. Joan asked.

"No, I don't have any set plans. I was just going to grab a taxi and explore around town a little bit."

Joan smiled. "Oh, maybe Malachi would be willing to show you around town today."

Kim needed to think fast. She was attracted to Malachi, and she didn't know if she would be able to keep her hands off of him. She had woken up twice last night from dreaming about his body. "Oh, I'm fine. I am pretty sure he has a lot to do today with his job."

"Today is my day off actually, and I would love to show you around." Malachi could see what his aunt was doing. She was setting him up on a date. That's why she invited him over to fix somethings. He knew if Kim said yes he wouldn't be able to say no. And he was going to take the bait because Kim was an attractive woman, and there was something about her that he wanted to know more about. "How bout we eat first and then we could head out?"

Kim didn't want to be rude, plus Malachi was handsome. "Sounds great." Kim fixed her plate and sat down. As soon as she sat down, Joan said she had some things to do around the place. Kim felt as if she was being set up on a date. It was strange that all of a sudden Malachi and her happened to run into each other again. Malachi was speaking, his voice was deep with such great authority. She could get lost in his words.

"Hello anybody in there?" he chuckled. "I was

saying how we have just been played by my aunt."

Kim couldn't believe she had just been caught staring. "It looks that way."

Kim ran back up to her room and grabbed her jacket. She couldn't believe that she was going around town with Malachi. She left her room and went back downstairs to meet with him.

"So Kim, what would you like to do today?"

"I really don't know. I just want to see the town and see what Atlanta has to offer."

"I got the perfect place, we can go horseback riding and my lovely aunt has prepared us a picnic basket for lunch."

"Oh wow, okay. Well this should be lovely, let's go." Kim never been on dates but she needed to see how Malachi was. He was her last chance at hope and sending her father away. That's why she was willing to go on a date with him.

Jasmine Barton-Moore

Chapter 7

KIM AND MALACHI WERE DRIVING in the car listening to music. Kim didn't know if she should start the conversation first. She was a little scared to start it. So, she just sat there nervously and twiddled her thumbs.

"So Kim, do you have any siblings? And tell me a bit about your parents? I feel like you know more about me than I know about you." He looked at Kim, waiting for an answer.

This is why Kim didn't want to get too close to anybody, she didn't want them poking around in her personal life. But she remembered that she needed the help from the Hopkins family. She just didn't know the right way to go about it. "Let's see... I have one sister, and my mom is deceased. I don't like to really talk about it."

"I understand." Malachi didn't want to push her any further. "Well, here's the place."

Kim was actually excited, she had never been on a horse before.

"Hey Jimmy, how is it going?"

"It's going great Malachi, I have those two horses

you wanted right over here."

"Thanks man, you're the best. Oh by the way, this is Kim."

Jimmy stuck his hand out. "Nice to meet you Kim."

"Same." Kim was trying to keep a low profile. The less people knew about her, the safer they would be. Kim looked over Jimmy, he didn't look all that bad. He was an older gentlemen missing a few teeth in his mouth.

Malachi took Kim's hand into his own and began walking toward the horses.

"Are you ready for this Kim?"

"As ready as I will ever be."

Malachi helped Kim up onto the horse and made sure she was situated before he got onto his. He also had the picnic basket with him. He knew the perfect spot to take them.

Chapter 8

THEY RODE SIDE BY SIDE IN SILENCE. Malachi was still trying to figure Kim out. He knew that he was attracted to her, but it seemed like she was holding out on him when it came to sharing details about herself. Or maybe it was just him being a paranoid detective. But there was this certain look on her face. She always seemed in deep thought or scared.

Kim could tell that Malachi was studying her every move. She didn't know if she should be afraid that he was trying to figure her out, but at this moment she had to put her fear aside because she needed someone to trust. All she knew was that she couldn't run forever. She decided to open up a little bit. She could stay close to the truth but didn't have to tell the whole truth. For some reason, with Malachi she felt safe. "My baby sister's name is Ava. She was named after our mother. She doesn't live with me at the moment. That part I rather leave out. My mom has passed away, I have never been married, or had children. That about sums it up for me."

Malachi couldn't believe that she decided to open

up, but she was so blunt about it. It was like she wanted to show emotion but didn't know how.

"Thank you for sharing that bit of information with me. You're doing great on that horse over there. Have you ridden before?"

"No, me and animals have always had a great connection." As she said that Kim reached out and patted the horse on his head.

Malachi chuckled, "Is that right?"

Kim could get used to his laugh. "It's true, I promise you."

"I believe you Kim. Well, looks like we are here." Malachi got off of his horse and helped Kim off of hers.

"It's beautiful Malachi." Kim walked over the edge. You could see the whole city from up here.

Kim stood sideways, and this gave Malachi the opportunity to study Kim's body. Kim was tall and slender, he couldn't get over her creamy mocha skin color. She had a beautiful face that went perfectly with her long neck. He moved down to her bosoms. She had the most perfect breasts, not too much but just enough to fit in the palm of his hands; if he ever had a chance to touch them. Her tummy was flat and long, she had wide hips and a nice round bottom. Her clothes fit her just right. There was something that just didn't sit right with him. He didn't know if it was because of a cop thing. Or it could be because his divorce ended badly and he hadn't been in a serious relationship since then.

Kim turned around and caught Malachi looking at her. She turned her face away and blushed a little. She had never had a guy pay that much attention to her. She turned back around and said, "Shall we start the picnic? I'm hungry."

Malachi didn't notice that Kim had started talking to him again. So, he was a little embarrassed when she started laughing at him. "Yes, let's start the picnic." He was caught staring for the second time. He laid the blanket down. He sat down and began to take out the food. He looked over at Kim. "You're welcome to sit down anytime, I won't bite, I promise."

Kim looked over at Malachi. She walked over and sat down. "This smells really good, I wonder what your aunt made."

"Let's see." Malachi pulled out meatloaf, candied yams, rolls, butter, and two slices of chocolate cake. "Yes, my aunt has shown out." Malachi fixed both of their plates and passed Kim hers. "Kim, what brings you to the ATL?"

Kim didn't know how she was going to respond to that question. She felt in her bones that he was a genuine person and wouldn't do her any harm. She could never be too safe, though. No matter what, she always had to protect herself and the people around her, so she decided to play it safe. "I came out here to do research on a person, but at the moment I cannot talk about it."

"So you're a reporter?"

"Not exactly, it's kind of personal research. And I rather leave it at that."

"Oh, okay got it. I won't push anymore. How are you enjoying your food?"

"This is really good, I remember growing up and watching my mom cook us food."

"That's good my aunt can cook. Before she opened a bed and breakfast she owned a restaurant in her younger days as she likes to say."

"Amazing." They sat in silence as they continued to finish their food. When they were done, Malachi packed everything up and placed it back into the basket. They sat there and enjoyed the scenery and breeze. The trees were swaying back and forth. And Kim could feel the air flowing through her hair. Kim wished that she could open up, but she just didn't trust anyone. She was starting to think this was a bad idea. "Malachi, I think I am ready to go back to the hotel now."

Malachi didn't know where that came from. He thought they were having a good time. But without hesitation he said, "Of course. Your wish is my command." They packed up everything and headed for the car.

Chapter 9

WHEN THEY ARRIVED BACK TO THE HOTEL, Malachi turned to Kim and said, "I would like to do this again Kim." Kim looked down and twiddled her fingers. Her eyes was telling him no. She had this scared look on her face. So, Malachi said something before she could respond. "I know there are certain things you do not want to talk to me about. And I am okay with that until the time is right, but I haven't been attracted to a woman since my divorce. There is something about you that I want to get to know, I am curious to see where this is going to take us." Kim looked into Malachi's eyes. He was being genuine with his words. Kim was still unsure about his offer, but what could be the worse thing to happen. Plus she needed someone to trust. "Okay Malachi, let's give it a shot."

That's all Malachi needed to hear. "Okay then, let's go to the movies tomorrow." Malachi knew that he needed to make the date fast before Kim changed her mind on him.

Kim was hesitant at first. She thought they would see each other in a couple of days -- not tomorrow. But she liked Malachi and said she would try. "If we can schedule it for 6pm, then you have yourself a date. Because I am supposed to have lunch with your sister tomorrow.

"Deal."

Malachi got out of the car and walked over and opened Kim's door. She stepped out and they continued to walk toward the hotel together. "See you later Kim." He leaned in and gave her a kiss on the cheek.

Kim smiled and said, "Goodbye."

* * *

After Kim got out of the shower, she called her best friend Tommy. "How is everything Kim? Did you find what you were looking for? I think time is running out."

"Yes, I think I have. I am trying to figure out how to present the case to them. I wish you were here with me."

"Kim you will figure it out, you know it is not safe. I can protect you better if we keep our distance and conversations to a minimum. We shouldn't even be on the phone right now."

"I know. Well, I am going to head to sleep."

"Goodnight Kim, it's almost over, I promise."

"Okay." Kim hung up the phone with Tommy. She thanked God for him each and every day. If it wasn't for him she would probably be dead already.

She didn't tell him about Malachi because she wanted to see where that would go since she was so attracted to him. She closed her eyes and hoped that tonight she would dream of happy thoughts.

* * *

The next morning Kim woke up feeling refreshed. She didn't have one of her nightmares, she actually dreamed about Malachi. She had dreamed that they were in her hotel bed making love. She couldn't believe she had dreamed that. She smiled and got up to take her shower.

* * *

Nia would meet her around noon. She went down to the breakfast hall and saw Mrs. Joan setting up. "Good morning Mrs. Joan."

"Good morning sweetie, how did you sleep?"

"That was the best sleep I have gotten in awhile." Kim was being honest about her sleep. Last night was the first time since her mom passed where she was able to sleep peacefully.

"Well, that is good to hear. How did your date go with my nephew yesterday?"

Kim smiled at her. "It went well, we plan on going to the movies tonight."

"That's good. Well, I will let you enjoy your breakfast. I'll see you later."

"See you later."

Kim sat in peace. She could finally concentrate on

what she needed to get done. First she needed to hack into the Atlanta police station to see if they had any information regarding her biological father. Kim was aware of the FBI in Atlanta because she overheard Malachi and his partner discussing the case over the phone. Malachi didn't say much, but apologized for having to take the phone call. Kim was good at what she did. She kept little magnifying trackers in her purse. You could attach it to any phone or leave it in a car. It could collect someone's whole life just with a click of a button on her cell phone. She felt bad for deceiving Malachi, but she had to get her mom justice.

Kim went back to her room and immediately got to work. She had gotten everything she needed from the police data reports. She knew exactly why the FBI were there. Now she just needed to stay close to Malachi but keep a low profile at the same time. She decided she was going to lay down and read a book until Nia arrived.

* * *

Malachi couldn't get Kim out of his mind. It was something in him that made him want to be closer to Kim. He hadn't felt this way about a women in a long time. He ran a few errands before he pulled back up to the hotel to pick her up for their date. It was about ten til' six. All he could do was think about kissing her lips and rubbing his hands all over her body. He needed to stop thinking about her because the bulge in his pants just kept getting bigger and bigger. He waited a few minutes until it went down before he got out of his car.

"Hey auntie how is it going?" He walked over to his aunt and gave her a hug and kiss on the cheek.

"It's going well, business is good as always. You're here to pick up Kim?"

"Yes ma'am."

"Well, let me buzz her for you then."

While waiting for Kim, Malachi decided to pull his phone out and play a game. He looked up because he heard the sound of heels, and his breath was knocked right out of him. Kim looked stunning. She was wearing a turtleneck dress in the color black that hugged her body and he could see every curve she had. Her shoes were open toed black heels. Her makeup was casual and her hair was in a messy bun, but it fit her face. It was her actual hair. He couldn't believe how beautiful she looked. He wondered why she didn't wear her natural hair more often. Her skin tone complemented her outfit. As Kim reached the bottom of the stairs she said, "Malachi are you ready to go?"

"Yes I am, you look beautiful by the way."

"Thank you, you look good yourself." Nia had talked her into getting this dress when they went out for lunch. Turns out Nia loves to shop, and once Kim mentioned her date with Malachi, Nia suggested that she buy it.

On the car ride to the movies, she remembered seeing the expression Malachi had on his face when she descended from the top of the stairs. It wasn't quite the reaction she thought she would get. Yes she knew she was attractive, but Malachi was a very handsome man. And the fact that she had never been intimate with a man before made her feel a bit anxious. As he drove, it gave her chance to study his features. He was wearing a navy-blue polo shirt with a pair of jeans that fit just right He had on a nice pair of navy-blue dress shoes. His hair had a fresh cut to it. She really liked his beard. He kept it clean and trimmed. His skin was a smooth chocolate color. He had to be at least six feet, maybe even taller. His eyes were almost as dark as his skin, but they were kind.

Chapter 10

AFTER, THE MOVIE HAD ENDED, they went back to Malachi's place for dinner. He wanted to impress Kim with his cooking skills. "Make yourself at home, Kim." Malachi walked over to his radio and turned on classical music.

"What's for dinner?"

"It's a surprise." Malachi just smiled at her because she gave him a blank stare that said she didn't really like surprises.

"Where is your restroom?" Kim asked.

"Down the hall to the left." Malachi pointed.

Kim walked down the hall to the restroom. She walked in and closed the door behind her. It was a simple guest bathroom the colors were neutral colors. He stuck to beige and white, it was really coordinated. She wondered if he did it himself. She didn't have to use the restroom, but she needed time to pull herself together. She didn't know what would happen between her and Malachi tonight. When he told her that he would cook dinner for her, she was actually very surprised. That he was a man who could cook, because she did not know how to cook. She looked at herself in the mirror, and for the first time in a while she looked happy. Before heading out, she caught a glance at the mirror which cause her to smile before she headed back out. Kim heard her stomach growl. "It smells really good in here," Kim said.

"Thank you. Cooking runs in the family."

"I see." Kim looked at Malachi, he had on his chef hat and apron on.

Malachi poured Kim a glass of Stella Rose red. Kim took her drink and walked over to the couch to have a sip. As she looked around the room, she noticed his leather couches. A flat screen television that was hanging against the wall. There was a huge collection of records lined up. His living room looked masculine, but she really liked the color scheme he had going on. It was filled with beige, black and white.

"Dinner will be ready in ten minutes," Malachi said.

Kim waited patiently as Malachi finished prepping dinner. As she listened to the classical music she thought back to her childhood. She felt the back of her eyes burning and the tears wanting to fall down, so she immediately came back to the present. She heard Malachi say, "Dinner is served." She got up from the couch and walked over to the table. He had lit some candles and dimmed the lights. He walked over and pulled her chair out. He's a true gentleman she thought to herself.

She sat down and looked at all the food. "Wow Malachi, this is really amazing." He made baked lemon chicken with fresh lemon peels as garnish. It was accompanied by green beans, mashed potatoes, rolls, sweet potato pie and of course a bottle of wine. "When did you have time to prep all of this?"

"Well, I knew I wanted to cook for you when you mentioned that you hadn't had a home cooked meal in a long time. So, I thought why not show off my skills."

Kim was shocked that he paid so much attention to such a small detail like that. "How sweet Malachi, and I am truly thankful."

"Don't thank me just yet, let's try the food first, shall we?"

"Of course." Malachi fixed Kim's plate and sat it in front of her. He watched as she bit into the chicken. Who knew that watching a woman eat chicken would be such a turn on for him. He watched as she closed her eyes and began to chew. Some of the broth drpped down her lip. He wanted nothing better to do than to walk across the table and lick the broth from her lips. He didn't know what had gotten into him. Kim was different, she was special to him, and he couldn't quite explain it yet. Kim opened her eyes and saw Malachi staring at her, so she smiled.

"So Kim, what do you think of my chicken?"

"This is absolutely amazing."

"I am glad to hear that."

"I have no idea why you even doubted yourself in the first place."

"It's not so much doubt but more of who I am trying to please."

Kim just looked at him and said, "OH."

They finished their meals and both got up to clear the table. Kim felt it was only right to help since he had cooked such a delicious meal for her. After they were finished cleaning up, they headed toward the living room. Malachi turned on the slow jams from his phone. "Kim, do you want to dance?"

Kim didn't really have much to lose by dancing. She walked over to him, put her hands around his neck, and gently laid her head on his shoulder as they began to move to the music. Kim felt so safe with him. They danced through three songs. Malachi lifted Kim's head from his shoulder. "Kim, may I kiss you?"

Kim looked into his eyes and she could feel the connection. She nodded her head yes. Malachi tilted his head to the side and leaned in. He placed his lips over her's. He began moving his hand up and down her body. A part of Kim wanted to stop him, but the other part of her wanted him to continue. She was tired of living in the dark and not being able to be satisfied as a woman. He wanted her, and she wanted him. He put his hands on her butt and pulled her in closer. Kim heard a moan escape from herself.

Malachi stopped kissing her and looked into her eyes. Kim nodded, giving him the okay to continue. Malachi unzipped her dress and she stepped out of it. He walked her over to the couch and proceed to remove her heels. He began to undress himself. He stood in front of Kim completely naked. Kim's mouth went dry. Malachi gently laid Kim back and climbed on top of her; he began to kiss her lips again. He moved his hand down to her hidden treasure. He could feel the hairs on his palm that were protecting her hidden treasure. He found her clit and began to play with it as he inserted a finger inside of her. She was a little tight, but he thought nothing of it. He began thrusting his finger in and out. Kim arched her back so that Malachi could go deeper. Kim didn't know what was happening, all she knew was she felt an instant release; it was like she was floating on cloud nine. Malachi leaned down and kissed her then he moved down further, putting his mouth over her breast. He moved down to her hidden treasure and then placed his mouth there. He licked her clit and put his tongue inside of her. He began speeding up. He could feel her on the verge of climaxing, so he removed his mouth, climbed on top of her, and grabbed a condom from his side dresser and unwrapped it and covered his shaft. He kissed her on the lips as he entered inside of her.

Malachi froze; it couldn't be possible. He looked down at Kim. Her face showed no expression. "Kim, are you a virgin?"

Kim looked at Malachi. She didn't know what to say or how to respond. So, she thrust up, taking him all the way in. It pained her a little, but she kept moving. Malachi gritted his teeth and finally began to move with her. He couldn't hold out any longer.

Kim never felt this free before in her life. She felt that tightening feeling in her gut again and she screamed out Malachi's name, and Malachi followed right behind her. He looked at Kim. "You should have told me." He pulled out of her, looked down and realized the condom broke. "Shit!" he said before he got up and left. The next thing Kim heard was the shower running. She was a little hurt and didn't know what to do, so she got dressed and left. Kim cried the whole way back to her room. She was too tired to shower, so she just put on a t-shirt and climbed into bed.

Chapter 11

"BOSS, I THINK WE FOUND HER."

"Where is she?" James asked.

"She is in Atlanta. You were right. We followed her friend, and she eventually called him and we were able to trace the phone call back to a hotel room."

"Good, you guys head up first and check it out. When everything looks safe, give me a call."

"Okay boss."

James was one step closer to finding his daughter. She had finally slipped up. He gave the agent a call. "Agent Burns, I found her."

"Do you not know what time it is James?"

"I don't care about the time, you work for me, remember."

Agent Burns couldn't argue there because he was holding her son hostage. "Where is she?"

James gave her the address and hung up the phone.

* * *

He knew he shouldn't have done that, but it felt so right.

Malachi got out of the shower and went downstairs. He needed the shower to clear his mind and think about what he was going to say to Kim. He looked around the whole house to realize that she had actually left. He ran back upstairs to put on clothes and drove to the hotel. If his mom found out how he just treated Kim, she would have a heart attack.

* * *

Kim woke to someone knocking on her door. She looked at the clock that was on the night stand. It read four AM. She had left Malachi's house just an hour ago. She rolled out of bed and grabbed her robe from the edge of the bed then walked over to the door. She opened it without checking who it was first. And there he stood. Kim was at a loss for words. She didn't know what to say because she wasn't expecting him to show up at her door. "Malachi, what are you doing here?"

"I could ask you the same question Kim. You're the one who left in the middle of the night."

Kim just stared at him. She didn't expect him to call her out the way he just did. And she clearly didn't want everyone in the hallway to know her business. "Come in Malachi. You're the one who left to take a shower after we had sex."

Malachi stepped inside the room, sat his things down on the table, and pulled out a chair. He turned on the light at the table and looked at Kim. He could tell that she had been crying. Her eyes were red and puffy. He felt a sense of guilt because he knew that he was the reason she had been crying. He was not behaving like the true gentleman that his parents raised him to be. He stood up, walked over to the bathroom and started the bath water. Kim was confused, he came back out and took her hand in his and led her to the bathroom. He undressed himself again and pulled her t-shirt over her head. Kim was still confused, but she just stood there and let him. He lifted her into the tub and pulled her down into the lukewarm water. Her back against his chest. Kim was still in shock that Malachi had driven all this way to make sure she was okay. No one had ever done that for her since her mother had been murdered. "I told you that my life is complicated, and I cannot explain it to you. What we did was wonderful, but I cannot let it happen again."

"Why is it that we can't enjoy the here and now? Why do we have to think about the later? Here we are, two adults just enjoying ourselves."

"Malachi because all I'm trying to do is pass through."

"I see. Well I really did enjoy our time together, and I am sorry that we cannot move past your complications in life. I want to see more of you. I can't explain it just yet, but I need you."

Kim didn't know what to say to that. Should she test it out and see what happens? Or once he finds out, is he going to push her away? All she could do was wait and see.

"Malachi, I don't know what tomorrow holds or what will happen once you find out the truth about me, but I would also like to give us a chance."

Malachi turned her around to face him and kissed her on the mouth. "Now how come you never lost your virginity and failed to tell me you were a virgin?"

Kim didn't know how to respond to that. "I just never found the right person to lose it to."

Malachi didn't believe her and didn't want to push any further. "Let's get out of this tub before we turn into prunes."

Malachi got out the tub first and helped Kim out. He wrapped his arms around her waist and then around her body. He looked at Kim and kissed her on the forehead, nose, cheek, and then mouth. "Bedtime, Kim. It's been a long day for you."

Chapter 12

MALACHI SAT IN HIS CAR ON HIS way to work. He was still thinking about how he had caught Kim off guard when she opened the door and saw him standing there. There was something about Kim that he just couldn't put his finger on, but after last night he knew she was turning into someone very special to him. Malachi pulled into his parking spot and headed inside. He saw Willow sitting down at her desk, head deep into reading the case files. She had probably read through those files a million of times.

"Look who decided to show up to work today. I was beginning to worry about you, you're never late," Willow teased. "Did you meet a woman?"

"That's none of your business, I am not going to discuss my personal life with you."

"You've done it in the past, that must mean this girl is a something special."

Malachi could see the smirk on her face. "I have no comment on that. Here comes Agent Burns."

"Ugh, why does she have to be here."

"What you need to do is stay out of my business

and play nice. I don't know why you don't like agent Burns. She's done nothing to you."

"I know, but she seems so uppity. And plus something just doesn't seem right with her, she gives off bad vibes."

"Good morning detectives, would you guys mind following me into the Chief's office? I have a new lead on the case."

"Yeah, let's go Willow." Willow gave Malachi a stern look.

Once inside the office, Agent Burns closed the door behind them. "I just got confirmation that James has sent people out here to look for a woman. We believe that she is his undocumented daughter."

"Well, where do we go from here?" Willow asked.

"We try and find out what his people know. We have one down in interrogation right now. We flagged his credit cards so anytime there was any action we would know where he was. So, we picked him up at a hotel and brought him in for questioning. Let's go. I will do the interrogating and you guys will watch."

"Why are you the only one allowed in the room to interrogate him?" Willow asked her.

Agent Burns wished Willow would just go with the flow and stop asking so many questions. Now she had to think quickly and lie once again to a fellow officer. "Detective Willow, we don't want to scare him off. You have to remember he works for one of the most dangerous men in California."

Willow just stared at her. There was still something about Agent Burns that she couldn't quite put her finger on, and it was annoying her. Malachi looked at Willow giving her a signal to be quiet. Malachi was the type of partner who did not voice his opinion too much, but he always had his guard up. So, she would trust him. "Fine let's go."

Agent burns entered the investigation room.

"Hello Mickey, I am Agent Burns with the FBI. I have a few questions to ask you."

"I have nothing to say to you pigs."Mickey was a little scruffy around the face like he hadn't slept in a couple of days. His eyes looked tired.

"I already know that you are out here looking for someone, so let's just speed up the process and you tell me who," Agent Burns said raising her voice. Agent Burns already knew the who, but she had to make it seem like she was asking the right questions. And not let the others know that she knew more than what she knew. She knew about Mickey, but he didn't know anything about her. She did everything for her son. She just wanted him safe and home with her again.

Mickey sat still and said nothing.

"Okay, well let me take a guess. Are you out here looking for your BOSS'S daughter?" His blank expression immediately changed; it was a dead giveaway. "It looks like I am onto something, thank you for that information."

"I didn't say anything!" Mickey screamed.

"But your face did. You see with criminals, they don't know how to keep a straight face, and that my friend is why you are a pawn and will never be the boss."

"You bitch!" Mickey yelled at her as she was walking out the door.

"So how do we find her?" Willow asked.

"I have yet to figure that out, but based off the bit of information we do know, it has to be someone who is simply passing through town and has not been here too long. That is where we should start."

Malachi's mind instantly went to Kim, but he let the idea slip away just as quickly as it came.

* * *

Agent Burns went into the ladies' room. She checked all the stalls and then instantly began to cry. She knew that Mickey was in town, James had told her that night he called. She couldn't wait to be out of this mess and have her life back. She spent most of her days looking over her shoulder, and James made it crystal clear that he could get to her son anytime he wanted. Her husband used to work for James. She never asked too many questions because he was bringing in a lot of money to the point where she didn't have to work anymore. Come to find out, her husband ripped James off and fled the country, leaving her to clean up his mess. Now his debt was her own and she was James's little puppet in the FBI. She wished she could tell someone, but James had eyes all over the place. She made sure that any case built against James didn't surface. She tampered with evidence and made witnesses disappear. He had just recently taken her son because she refused to do any more jobs for him. She had been doing this for a good two years now. She didn't know how long she could keep lying to theses detectives, especially with detective Fox watching her every move.

Sometimes she hated being a cop. Her sole purpose of joining the FBI was to help people. And now here she was at the age of thirty-three working for one of the largest crime bosses in the state of California. She just wanted out, but she had to do this for her son's sake. She hadn't seen her son in three months, but sometimes James would let her talk to him on the phone. He was scared but he was being a brave little boy for mommy. She looked at herself in the mirror, wiped her eyes, applied some makeup and walked out the bathroom.

Jasmine Barton-Moore

Chapter 13

MALACHI WAS FINALLY OFF OF WORK, and all he could think about was rushing home to clean up and have dinner with Kim. He wanted nothing more than to protect her from the world that she was lost in. He made it home and walked straight to the shower. They had decided that she would take a taxi to his house to have dinner and talk. He wanted to pick her up, but she had insisted on grabbing a taxi.

Kim stood outside of Malachi's door contemplating if she wanted to ring the doorbell. She knew that she liked him more than any other guy. Well, technically he was the only guy she had slept with. She decided not to be a coward and rang it. She waited for him to come to the door. When he opened the door, he was like a breath of fresh air. She could tell that he had just stepped out of the shower because there were drops of water dripping from his hair.

"Come in."

Kim entered his house and immediately smelled the food that he had prepared. "You're going to have to stop making all these meals for me. I have to keep figure," Kim said jokingly.

"I think your body looks perfect." Malachi looked her up and down and instantly thought back to last night. "Well, I hope you brought your appetite."

"Always," Kim replied. She could eat some food, especially some good home cooking.

They sat down and enjoyed each other's company over their dinner. After clearing the table and washing the dishes, they made their way over to the couch to sip on some wine.

"The food was amazing like always Malachi. How was work?" Kim asked.

"Thank you, and it was good. We are about to close a major case."

Kim knew what that case was because she had hacked into his computer system when she got here. So every time he logged into his computer, the information from his computer would download to hers, and she could do any of that from all the computers in the department. She knew that her father and now the cops were looking for her, and she was running out of time. The first time in her life she didn't know what to do, but it was like she needed Malachi in her life.

"That's good."

"I don't want to talk about work. I can't explain it, but I am attracted to you and I want you in my life."

Kim just looked at Malachi she didn't know what

to say. "Malachi, you know where I stand on the whole relationship thing. I just can't; there are things I can't tell you because if you knew, you would despise me. Remember we're just having fun."

Malachi knew she spoke the truth, but he couldn't lose her. Plus how bad could it really be. Being with Kim was different than being with his ex-wife. He needed Kim like he needed his next breath of air, but he wasn't going to tell her that. She needed time. He looked at her and watched as she bit her bottom lip. He loved when she did that, he knew that was her in deep thought. He leaned in and kissed her on her lips to silence her.

Kim was at a loss for words because here was a man who was willing to be with her even though he didn't know the truth. Should she trust her feelings? She was tired of having no one to really lean on, and he did say it didn't matter whatever the truth was. She went with her gut and continued to kiss him back.

Malachi couldn't control himself. He began removing Kim's clothes. Then he immediately took his off. He grabbed a condom and covered his shaft. "Am I moving too fast for you, Kim."

Kim looked at Malachi. "Not at all."

He kissed her one last time, then turned her around, and entered inside of her. Kim had to place her hands on the wall so she wouldn't lose her balance. Malachi began to move inside of her. Kim couldn't believe how good he felt inside of her. Malachi made her feel complete. She needed him like she needed air to breathe.

Malachi pulled out, picked Kim up, and made his way to the bedroom. He laid her on the bed and entered her once again. He began to move back and forth in slow motion. Kim wrapped her legs around his waist then wrapped her arms around his strong neck. Malachi began whispering sweet things into her ear. How much he wanted to be with her and that he would protect her. Kim could feel herself on the verge of coming. She pulled Malachi closer to her and she could feel him getting deeper inside of her. She began to scratch his back and whimper. "Malachi, I'm about to come!"

Malachi lifted her an inch off of the bed and began to speed up the process. Kim threw her head back and that was Malachi's undoing. Once he saw her hair laid out on the pillow and her moaning, he let it all out. Kim followed right behind him letting everything go; the built-up anger from her mom's death, the fact that her own father wanted her dead, the fact that she was on the run and couldn't be with her sister or best friend. The love she had for Malachi, but knew he would hate her as soon as he found out the truth. The tears had begun falling and she didn't even realize it until Malachi said something.

"Hey baby, are you okay?"

Kim couldn't speak. She didn't know when it had happened, but she had fallen in love with a man who knew nothing about her but was willing to give his all. Kim wiped her tears away and said, "I am fine, I just never felt the way I just felt at that moment."

Malachi looked down at her and couldn't tell if she was telling the truth. He pulled her closer to him, then kissed her on the cheek. "Everything will be alright, Kim. I got you. Close your pretty little eyes and sleep."

Kim leaned into him and cried even harder. She eventually fell asleep in his arms.

* * *

The next morning Malachi woke up before Kim and was pleased to see that she was still sound asleep next to him. He thought back to last night when they decided to continue their love making upstairs. Then after resting for an hour they went back at it. Malachi heard his doorbell ring and looked over at the clock. It was six am, so he was wondering who it was. He heard it again. He hurried up and put on some clothes before whoever it was woke up Kim. He opened the door and there his brothers, sister, and partner stood. Something had to be up because they were all there really early. "What the hell are you guys doing at my place so early?"

"We need to talk to you about Kim," Mia said.

"There is nothing to talk about Mia, I already know that Kim has a troubled past."

"Yeah, but do you know how troubled?" This time it came from Willow.

"No, I do not, but when she is ready to talk I am here for her."

"Bro you have fallen head over heels for her and you know nothing about her past," Malik said.

This was true, but he still needed to live his own life.

"Well, let us show you something about your so-called girlfriend." Willow barged in and began pulling out things from an envelope. "So you remember our meeting from Agent Burns yesterday. Well, I ran Kim's photo through our computer system and got a hit."

"You did what? What the hell Willow."

"Sorry Malachi, you would have done the same thing. She is the only new person I could think of who has come to town and doesn't really have a story. But anyways, come to find out James has sent his goons out here to look for Kim. It's his daughter."

Malachi was soaking everything in, he couldn't believe it. He knew he should have listened to his gut. "That just means that she is scared and that is why she is running from him."

"Well get this, I checked your activity from your account and saw that someone had access to it while you weren't even in the office. When I checked the times, it would be random times that your files were being accessed. Like three or four in the morning. They went above and beyond to cover their tracks, but since we upgraded our system a few months back, we can still go back in and track activity. We need to bring her in and ask her some questions."

At this point Malachi was furious. At that moment he heard a noise behind him and saw that Kim was standing there in his t-shirt.

"Malachi, what is going on?" Kim couldn't read his facial expression, but his was face was harsh. She could tell he was angry about something.

"How could you lie to our family like this?" Nia asked her.

Kim was confused. "I am sorry, I don't know what you are talking about." She knew what they were talking about but she needed to think of something to cover herself. Kim felt so weird just standing there in Malachi's shirt and he wasn't even saying anything to her.

"Oh stop the act Kim, we know who your father is. We know you used Malachi's code to hack into the police database."

Kim couldn't believe that everything was catching up with her. She couldn't believe she led herself to live in this fairy tale life with Malachi and now it was all coming to an end. Her past was catching up to her present. Malachi looked at Kim and saw her emotions, but she had quickly gathered her composure. "By your facial expression I am taking that this is all true then

Kim." Malachi asked.

"Malachi you don't understand, I told you before we got involved you wouldn't understand."

"Yes, but I could lose my job and everything I have worked for because you hacked into the system. You should leave Kim."

"Malachi, please."

He could tell that she was going to lose her emotions, but he didn't care. This was too much to handle. "I said get out!"

The sound of Malachi yelling at her made her jump. She walked over to the door and put on her sandals and grabbed her purse. She didn't dare go back upstairs and put on her own clothing. She looked back one more time at Malachi for reassurance and anger showed all over his face, She opened the door and left.

She stepped outside and the tears began to fall. How could she let herself get so emotionally involved with a man? She was thinking so hard about Malachi she didn't even notice the car coming up beside her. One guy hoped out, put something over her mouth and threw her in the trunk.

Chapter 14

MALACHI WAS STILL VERY UPSET, but he couldn't get Kim's face out of his head when she looked at him one last time. She had to be cold with only his t-shirt on. Well, he didn't care because he was angry. Everyone had come over to his place by then. His dad, mom, aunt, uncle, and agent Burns. They were talking about going after Kim and bringing her in. His mom and aunt were curious as to why he let her go, but he had no answer for them. He was hurting on the inside. \

He heard a knock on his room door and it was his mom.

"Mom I really don't feel like talking right now."

"I understand, that's why you're just going to sit there and listen. Now I know I am not a cop, but everything that I have heard today shows me that Kim is not a bad person. She just got caught up in a sticky situation. I can tell that you are in love with her by the way you are behaving. You should follow your heart and go find her. I know your dad taught you to be a cop first, but sometimes you have to be happy yourself. You ended your divorce badly, son. You know, me and your father have a pretty funny story on how we met."

Malachi looked at his mom. "Really."

"Yes, really. I was living in a group home until I was about twenty-five. He would patrol the streets I lived on. Long story short, he tried saving me from going down the wrong path, but I didn't want saving. I felt as if everyone around me had given up on me, but through it all, he stuck by me. He even locked me in jail just to keep me safe from the people I was hanging around. But of course at the time I didn't see it as keeping me safe. I saw it as him trying to keep me from my friends. So you see son, we all have a story to tell."

"Thanks mom, I didn't know that." He heard the doorbell ring again. He was tired of hearing that sound. He walked downstairs with his mom. At the door stood a girl who looked exactly like Kim, but she couldn't be any older than sixteen.

"May I help you?" Malachi asked.

"Yes, my name is Ava and I am looking for my older sister Kim." Nobody said a thing.

Malachi's mom finally said, "Hi, I am Katherine. Now let me get this straight, you said your sister? By the way, how old are you my dear?"

"I am sixteen. Kim hasn't checked in today, so I know something is wrong. As she paced back and forth. She told me that she had finally found the right cop family to bring her father to trial."

"Come in dear, now what do you mean trial?" Katherine asked.

"We have been on the run since that monster murdered our mother in front of Kim. Kim has been moving around trying to find cops to help us out, but every time Kim would hack into the system, she would find out that they were dirty and on the payroll of her father. So, we would move onto the next state. We've never travelled together because Kim said it is too dangerous, but she always let me know where she was. She said that our cover story would be that we lived in different countries so know one would ever put two and two together. But today she missed her check in with me, so I instantly knew something was wrong. Have you seen her?"

"Yes sweetie, but she left this morning. Have you tried her cell?"

Malachi couldn't believe his ears. Kim was in trouble and he just let her walk out the door.

"That's not how we work." Ava glanced around and saw the information of her sister scattered on the table. "I have to go."

Katherine saw what Ava noticed, it was photos of Kim's father and a few of Kim. "It's not what you think Ava."

"Not what I think? My sister was here and now she is not. Maybe she was wrong about you guys."

Ava was getting ready to leave when Malachi

blocked her path.

"Your sister was here and some things went down which caused her to leave because I was angry that she lied to me. But please let me help you find her." Ava had no other choice but to stay. Her sister said she could trust this family and she had know clue where her sister was. She went over to the table and pulled out her laptop and cell phone. She proceeded to turn on both devices with the hopes of tracking Kim. Everyone began introducing themselves. She knew who Malachi was because Kim had showed her a picture of him, and sent everything she was working on over to her to also. He walked over to her and asked what she was doing. So, she explained to him about the tracking devices.

Chapter 15

WHEN KIM WOKE UP, SHE DIDN'T know exactly where she was. All she could remember was one moment she was leaving Malachi's house and the next she had something covering her mouth. She tried to concentrate on the things around her. She could hear the sound of water moving and hitting the walls so, she figured that she was on a boat or somewhere near water.

They had taken her purse so she had no phone, but she looked down and noticed that her bracelet was still on her wrist. She knew that she had missed her check in with her sister, so it was just a matter of time before Ava came looking for her. All she had to do was stay alive.

Kim heard voices outside her door. She could see the knob turning and in walked her dad and Tommy. Tommy's face was all bruised up. She was so confused. She tried reading Tommy's expression, but she got nothing. All she could tell was that he had been beaten. She could see the pain and sorrow that filled his eyes.

"I have finally got you in my hands. This dumb

idiot led me straight to you."

Kim looked at Tommy. Her eyes big and confused as if he had given her up, but she knew Tommy would never do that to her.

"He led me straight to you, all I had to do was follow his routine. I instantly knew when you called him. I eventually got a tap on your location. You know it was always so difficult to find you because you were constantly moving. But for some reason you decided to stay in Atlanta. It was a man. A detective, am I right?"

Kim looked at him with such shock, she thought to herself, "How on earth did he know that?"

"What you fail to realize is that there are people all around you who work for me. Money can buy anything. And if money can't buy them, then I take further measures. I have someone currently working for me at that department. You thought that you could get away from me, didn't you? Your mother got away from me once, and I am not letting that happen again. Well, Tommy, I want to thank you for your services." He pointed the gun at the back of Tommy's head and pulled the trigger and Tommy's body hit the ground.

Kim began screaming and pulling at the cuffs around her wrist. Trying to get her hands out of the cuffs.

"Now that that's all settled, we will be on our way out of the country. I can either sell you for profit, but if you cooperate, then you will work for me."

"You bastard, I hate you!"

"Good, I hate you too. Remember you were never supposed to be born." He slammed the door and left.

Kim looked at Tommy's lifeless body on the ground. Blood was gushing out of his head so quickly. She looked at his face and saw the tears that stained his skin. This was all her fault. She couldn't help but think she was really all alone in this world.

* * *

Malachi was happy because they had finally pinned Kim's cell phone and tracked her location to a boat. From the direction it was headed it looked like they were heading to Mexico. They prepared to bust the boat by calling in every police officer and FBI agency around. They also gave Agent Burns a ring since this was her case but not before locating the boat they couldn't really trust anyone. They arrived at the boat and put on the sirens. Someone began to open fire. By the end of the shootout some officers did get injured, but no one had died. All Malachi cared about was finding Kim.

Immediately after they rounded everyone up and placed them in handcuffs, they then searched the boat, bringing the paramedics with them. Malachi then came to a locked door. He and his officers kicked it in. Malachi walked through the door and saw Kim handcuffed to a rail. He saw a body laying directly in front of her. She looked scared and angry. He called her name but got nothing. He knew that she was lost in her own thoughts. He walked over and removed her handcuffs. The first thing she did was run over to Tommy. She kneeled next to him and shut his eyes. She got up and looked at Malachi and said, "I am ready." He led her by her hand as they exited the boat. Back at the dock she was checked out by the paramedics. They advised her to go to the hospital for further examination, so that's where they went. They rode to the hospital in complete silence.

Chapter 16

THEY ARRIVED AT THE HOSPITAL TO FIND everyone in the waiting room. Ava walked up to Kim and gave her a big hug. "Kim, what's the matter, is everything alright?" Kim looked pale in the face as if she was getting ready to pass out.

All Kim said was, "They killed Tommy." And then her world went black.

When Kim woke up again she was laying in bed with IV's in her arms. She glanced up and found Malachi's mom tidying up around the room. She must have sensed that Kim was up; she turned around and said, "Good morning."

"Good morning. How long have I been out, and where is my sister?" Kim said as she looked around the hospital room. It was your standard hospital room. It had a television in the corner and a window you could look out.

"Your sister is at my house, I told everyone that I would call when you woke up."

"Oh. What happened to me?"

"You blacked out. You were dehydrated Also, I

don't know how else to tell you this, but you're pregnant."

Kim wasn't sure if she heard her correctly. "Did you just say I'm pregnant? That's impossible." Kim did remember her and Malachi using protection, but he was also her first, so she wasn't quite too sure.

"Yes sweetie."

"Does Malachi know?"

"Yes, he does. He has been by your side this whole time. He rushed home to change, but he will be back in a few."

"Oh."

"I know what my children have said and done to you, but Malachi has a good heart, just give him a chance. You and your sister have both grown on me so much I would hate to lose you guys." Kim didn't have much to say. She couldn't believe her best friend was dead and that she was pregnant. She glanced toward the door and noticed Malachi standing there.

"Mom, can you give us a moment to talk?"

"Yes, of course my dear."

Kim looked at Malachi as he took the vacant seat his mom had just left. She looked down and started playing with her fingers.

"Kim, I know that I hurt you and I wasn't there for you when you needed me to be, but I know about the baby and I want us to make this work."

Kim didn't know what to say. She told him she

had secrets and he told her that they would deal with them when they crossed that bridge. But here he was asking her to make it work. She wasn't sure if she could open her heart again just to have it crushed. He hadn't even let her explain herself the last time. Kim looked at Malachi for a moment.

"At this time I do not want to talk about us, I want to focus more on making sure that my father is put in jail forever for killing Tommy and my mother."

Malachi was not expecting that answer, but he didn't want to push her away. "Okay, well who was Tommy to you?"

"He was my best friend and the only person who ever understood me. He has been there for me since the beginning. It's my fault that he is dead."

Malachi saw a tear fall from her eye. "It's not your fault Kim."

"How dare you say it's not my fault! You know absolutely nothing. I told you that there were certain things I couldn't tell you, and you told me that you were okay with that. Tommy is dead because I stayed here too long thinking we actually had something. But in reality, we had nothing. Malachi, please, I want you to leave."

Malachi was speechless. "Kim, I am sorry."

"Get out, get out now!" Kim began to shout.

In walked Kathleen. "What's going on Malachi? I see that you've upset Kim. I think you should leave."

Malachi looked at Kim and then back at his mom. He got up and left her hospital room.

Chapter 17

KIM WAS RELEASED FROM THE HOSPITAL the following day. Malachi's mom wanted Kim and Ava to stay with her, but it would be too difficult for her to look at Malachi. She hadn't really eaten anything since coming home from the hospital. Her sister offered her some food, but she just declined it. She knew that she should stay nourished, now that she was pregnant, but she wasn't in the mood to eat. Later that day she had an appointment to see the chief of police to bring in her evidence from her mom's death. She was hesitant to go because she knew she would see Malachi, but she wanted justice for her family.

Malachi knew that Kim was coming in and he didn't know what to do with himself. He hadn't spoken to her since the day she kicked him out of the hospital. Willow was saying something to him, but he was lost in his own thought.

"Malachi what's the matter?"

"Willow, you know what's wrong."

"Malachi, she will come around."

"You guys are the ones who came to my house

and instantly ruined everything. Kim is pregnant and wants nothing to do with me."

"So, you would rather have us not tell you? Your unbelievable Malachi." Willow got up and left.

Malachi knew he was being unreasonable. Malachi knew that if he was in Willow's shoes, he would have done the same thing because that's what partners do. "Wait Willow."

Willow turned around and glanced at him.

"I am sorry. You're right, I would have done the same thing if I knew you were in danger. It's just that Kim told me from the beginning that her life was complicated, and I told her that didn't matter. That I wanted to see where our relationship would take us. Now I find out that she's pregnant with my child and she can't even stand to look at me."

"I'm sorry partner." Willow walked over to Malachi and wrapped her arms around him.

"Thanks for the hug Willow, I needed that." Just as he unwrapped his arms from around Willow he could see Kim staring at them. He could see the expression of hurt splattered on her face, but she composed herself and headed straight to the chief's office.

Kim saw Malachi and Willow hugging. She didn't care, but yesterday he was asking for forgiveness but yet hugging the very women that came between their relationship. Even though it was difficult, she knew she loved Malachi. She knocked on the chief's door and waited for him to signal her to come in. "Good morning Kim, it's good to see you."

Kim just smiled and sat down.

"Kim, I know the things you went through will be hard for you to talk about, but we want to get justice for everyone he has hurt."

"I understand." Kim said.

"One last thing before we start, I would like to invite detective Malachi and detective Willow in here as witnesses. There is an FBI agent assigned to the case, but she is escorting the prisoner at the moment. I know you and Malachi have some things to work out, but I want you to know that he is one of our best detectives. He knows James's case inside and out.

Kim looked at the chief and captain then just said, "It's fine." She just wanted to make sure Tommy and her mom received the justice they deserved. The chief waved Malachi and Willow over to enter his office. Kim did not even bother to turn around when the two detectives entered the room.

"Kim, when you're ready," the chief said.

Jasmine Barton-Moore

Chapter 18

"I GUESS THE ONLY PLACE TO START IS from the beginning. From an early age my mom always knew that I was a genius. She enrolled me in dance classes, computer classes, you name it I was in it. I always felt so different compared to the other kids. Even though we lived in a big fancy house, I still attended public school. And that's when I met Tommy. I was seven years old when he came to our school. It was during lunch time and all the kids were standing around him because he had a hole in his shoe. So, they teased him about being poor. I went into my backpack and grabbed my scissors and I cut a hole in my shoe. I walked right up to the crowd of kids and asked if that had classified me as poor too. They all just stared at me and walked away. After everyone cleared out, I introduced myself to Tommy. He told me that I didn't have to do that because he could take care of himself. I told him that I knew that, but I believed that no one should be teased because they were less fortunate. Tommy just looked at me and walked away. I thought I made a friend that day, but apparently not. A few weeks later I noticed that during lunch time he would place food in his backpack, so one day I asked him about it and he told me to mind my own damn business. I remember telling him that if he was hungry he was more than welcome to share my lunch. My mom always packed more than enough food for me. From that day forth we became the best of friends.

"His dad was a real piece of work, he would hit Tommy and his mom. As we got older, my mom started travelling a lot more, so Tommy stayed at my house most nights. He ended up getting a full scholarship to college for football. Even though Tommy came from a broken family, he still had both parents. I remember wishing that I had a dad. My mom never talked about my father and I didn't know why. As she was away on trips I started doing research on my biological father. I found him, of course. I took a two hour train ride to see him. All I had to do was pull out cash my mom wouldn't have asked any questions. When I knocked on his door I was so excited to finally meet him. That was when he told me that I wasn't supposed to be born and that my mom was supposed to have an abortion.

I rushed home crying to my mom and told her everything, but by that time it was too late. My father had already followed me home. My mom made me hide, she told me to take the tunnel out, but I just had to see what he was going to do to her. He shot her, pointblank in the head. After I made sure my sister was secure in our getaway car, I went back to the house to gather evidence."

Malachi couldn't believe what he was hearing. He saw Kim reach down and grab a box. Kim continued speaking.

"In this box are the clothes my mom was wearing with her blood along with the weapon. My mom had already had our bags and passports ready. I guess she planned for this day all along. But I couldn't just leave my mom's body. It was my fault she was dead. I went to the airport and placed my sister on a plane, and I reassured her that I would shortly follow. I knew that I wouldn't, but I just said it so that she would feel better. Eventually she did come to live with me, but we did everything separately just so if we were being watched. I went back to the house and dialed 911. I don't know how it was possible, but my dad was able to make my mom's death disappear. I later found out that the cops were on the take. "I was about eighteen years old when my dad auctioned me off to the highest bidder out of spite." That's when the tears began to fall. He hated me so much that he sold me for one thousand dollars. The man who bought me was triple my age. If I had only listened to my mother and got on the airplane that night, I would not have been in that situation. Anyways, this man turned out to be very kind. He rescued girls like me who were in trouble. He taught me how to be a better hacker, and how to kill."

Malachi could listen no more. He got up and left the room. Willow followed behind him.

"What is the matter Malachi?"

"Listening to her story and seeing how that bastard treated his own flesh and blood like that, and then the way we have treated her."

"That's why we have to get back in there and make sure this bastard never sees the light of day again."

Malachi knew that Willow was right. He took a deep breath and said, "Let's go back in."

Chapter 19

KIM KNEW THAT MALACHI HAD STEPPED out, but she didn't know if it was something that she had said. She saw when detective Willow followed behind him. She needed to get Malachi out of her head and focus on her mother's and Tommy's cases.

"Kim, would you like to take a break?" Chief had asked her.

"No, I want to finish so I can put this behind me." She continued, "The guy I was sold to, I lived with him for a year. He was able to get me in contact with my sister. He knew that my dad was a bad person and he had daughters of his own. He only wanted the best for me, and he actually became my father figure. But all good things must come to an end. My biological father found out and had him killed. He had already taught me so much; he taught me how to move from place to place without getting caught. When it was no longer safe for me to live with him he gave me money and told me to leave. He also taught me to hide. As you probably know, Ava and I both wear similar tracking bracelets. I also got in contact with Tommy; I just wanted to talk to someone familiar. So ever since then, I have been on the run. Going from state to state, trying to find "good" cops that could help me.

"Well, we are going to take him down," said the chief. "If it comes down to it, are you willing to testify?"

Kim dug in her purse and pulled out a little black book. "I am not willing to testify. I would probably shoot him where he stood if I had the chance, but in this book I have every bit of information you need to put him away. Dirty cops on the take, from state to state. I did my part, now it is time for me to lay my friend to rest." Kim stood up. "If there is nothing else, I would like to return to my hotel room."

Everyone in the room stood up. "Thank you for this information. If we do have any questions, then we will contact you. My daughter Nia will be the attorney for this case."

Kim shook the chief's hand, she looked at Malachi and Willow, nodded then headed out.

"Malachi, are you not going to go after her?" Willow had asked.

"No, I rather put that bastard away and be the one to let her know we did.

Chapter 20

ONCE KIM GOT TO HER CAR, she broke down and cried. Everything she had said in there were things she wanted to forget, but this is why she did everything she needed to do. Just so that her mom would have justice. She knew what she had to do next, she needed to fly home for her friend's funeral. She knew that his body was already sent over. She hadn't talked to Tommy's mom because she didn't know exactly what to say to her. She would find out when she got there.

Kim and Ava arrived back in California for Tommy's funeral.

"Kim, are you ready for this?"

"Honestly Ava I am not, but me and Tommy had a pact. If anything was to happen to either of us we would be there for each other's family, no matter the outcome. I am going to go in there and hold my head up high and hope for the best." Ava grabbed ahold of Kim's hand as they entered the service.

Everyone turned around as they walked in, including Tommy's Mom. They took a seat in the back. Kim looked at Tommy who was nicely dressed as he lay in his coffin. Tommy's mom got up to speak. "Even though I wanted to hate you Kim, in reality you saved my son. You gave him chances and opportunities that I wasn't able to give him, and I want to thank you for that. Tommy gave me this video and he said if he anything were to ever happen to him to show it at his funeral. I was waiting for you to arrive."

Kim just looked at Tommy's mom and sat there patiently. The video began. Tommy had pretty much recorded their entire friendship. Kim began to cry. He had clips of her singing and dancing and the both of them being silly. He had videos of his bruises and her helping him out. At the end of his video, he said to her, "You promised after we caught your dad you would sing again. You would sing about joy and happiness. You also promised to sing at my funeral."

Kim began to laugh. This was true.

"Kim, can you come up here please?" Tommy's mom said.

Kim stood up and walked to the front. Tommy's mom gave her a hug and handed her the microphone. Kim knew the song that Tommy would have wanted her to sing. "I Will Always Love You" by Whitney Houston." By the time Kim was done everyone was in tears and clapping for an encore. At the back of the room she saw Malachi's whole family standing there. She hadn't spoken to them since the day she handed over all of the evidence. His mom tried reaching out, but she just couldn't handle it. She wondered if they had news regarding the case.

As Kim stood at the front singing a Whitney Houston song Malachi knew that he was willing to make it work with Kim no matter what or how long it took. She looked so beautiful up there. She was wearing nude pants and jacket with white heels and a white shirt. Her hair was loose around her face. He couldn't believe she was having his child. As she began to sing he saw the tears fall from her eyes. He wanted nothing more but to go to her. But he waited. When she was done she opened her eyes and they connected to his. She looked away and took her seat.

Once Kim sat down she gave Ava this look that she knew she invited Malachi's family. Ava just smiled at her and looked forward. "Kim that was beautiful, your mom would be truly proud of you." Tommy's mom said. After they were done at the funeral home it was time for them to put her friend down in the ground.

Jasmine Barton-Moore

Chapter 21

EVERYONE WENT BACK TO TOMMY'S mom's house for food. It was a little cramped. Malachi's mom was the first to come up to her and give her a hug.

"How are you holding up sweetie?"

"I guess I'm fine. I am honestly tired. I am ready to go lay down."

"Malachi can take you home and you guys can catch up on the case."

Before Kim could object, she had already waived Malachi to come over.

"Yes, mother."

"Malachi you know I hate when you call me that. Will you please escort Kim home?"

"Kim, is that alright with you?"

Kim wanted to object, but being pregnant really made her exhausted. "What about my sister? I know that she is going to want to stay."

"That is fine Kim, we can take her home for you." Said Mrs. King.

"Okay, well let me say goodbye to Tommy's mom and let Ava know that I am leaving. By the way we are staying in my childhood home."

Kim stepped away for a moment.

Malachi leaned in and kissed his mother on the cheek and said thank you. Kim returned and they left.

Malachi's mom knew that they both needed a little push. Her husband walked over and asked, "What are you smirking about? Are you playing matchmaker?" She just smiled at her husband and said, "A mother knows best."

* * *

On the ride to Kim's house they were both silent. Kim wasn't surprised Malachi knew where she lived. They pulled up to her house and got out. "This is where you live?" Malachi asked her.

"Yes, this is the house I grew up in and the house my mom was murdered in."

Malachi didn't know how to respond to that, so he just followed her to the door step.

"Would you like to come in Malachi?" He nodded his head yes and followed her in. "Are you hungry or anything?"

He knew that Kim was trying to avoid the obvious, but he asked, "Can we talk?"

"Sure, let's sit down. Any news on the case?"

"After we presented all the evidence to your father and his lawyer, they took the plea agreement we were offering. Life without parole. He will die in prison."

Kim was satisfied with that.

Malachi no longer wanted to wait. "Kim, I know that I hurt you and I am sorry for that. I love you and I can't see myself being with anyone else but you. I know what I and my family did was wrong, but I was caught off guard. You are about to be the mother of my child. If you want, we can live in Atlanta, or we can live out here in your home. I want to be where ever you and my child are."

Kim looked at Malachi. She knew that she loved Malachi, she just felt so hurt. Her friend Tommy had sacrificed his life for her happiness. "I love you too Malachi. I know everything that happened wasn't you guys' fault. I should have been honest from the start, but I didn't know who to trust. I don't want to live in this house. It has to many bad memories. I want to live in Atlanta with you."

Malachi looked around the house and saw that it had been kept up, but he could understand her not wanting to stay in the how. He was happy to hear that. He pulled out a ring and said, "Would you do me the honor of becoming Mrs. Malachi Hopkins?"

Kim couldn't believe it. She screamed, "YES!"

Malachi pulled her in closer and gave her a big kiss. "You have lost so much weight."

"Yeah, I haven't been eating"

"Well that will change since you are pregnant with my child."

Jasmine Barton-Moore

Epilogue

AFTER MOVING TO ATLANTA WITH MALACHI and her sister, come to find out she was actually pregnant with twins. So, they had to get a bigger home. They had a simple wedding. After her twins were born she started a nonprofit organization. She wanted to help women all across the globe who were being forced into marriage or relationships.

She looked on the monitor and saw her babies crying. So, she went to them. They were probably hungry. She sat in her rocking chair and began to feed one of them at a time.

Malachi entered the nursey and looked at her. "Have I told you how proud of you I am?"

"Yes, you have. Every day."

Malachi bent down and gave her a kiss. He liked coming home on his lunch break to help her with the twins and just to see her beautiful face.

"Is there anything I can help you with?"

"Yes, you can pick up your daughter and hold her until I am done feeding him. Your children are so demanding."

Malachi laughed hard. "Just like their mother." Malachi sat there and watched Kim feed his daughter.

"Malachi, you're starting to get that look in your eyes."

"What look would that be?" he said with a smirk. He knew the look. He wanted to make love to Kim and that's exactly what he did.

JASMINE BARTON-MOORE

was born and raised in San Diego, California. Traveling from coast to coast as a military spouse. She obtained her associate's degree in English. She plans to further her education in the near future. Jasmine spends her time as a full-time teacher and a full-time author. Needless to say, this is the first stepping stone in Jasmine's fiction career. Make sure to look out for some new books that will be published in the late fall and winter.

You can learn more at:

jasminebartonmoore.com
Instagram @jasminebarton_moore
Facebook @Jasmine Barton-Moore
Youtube @Jasmine Barton-Moore

www.ingramcontent.com/pod-product-compliance
Lightning Source LLC
Chambersburg PA
CBHW030553130626
46552CB00006B/2532